THE PRINCESS AND THE PEA-ANO

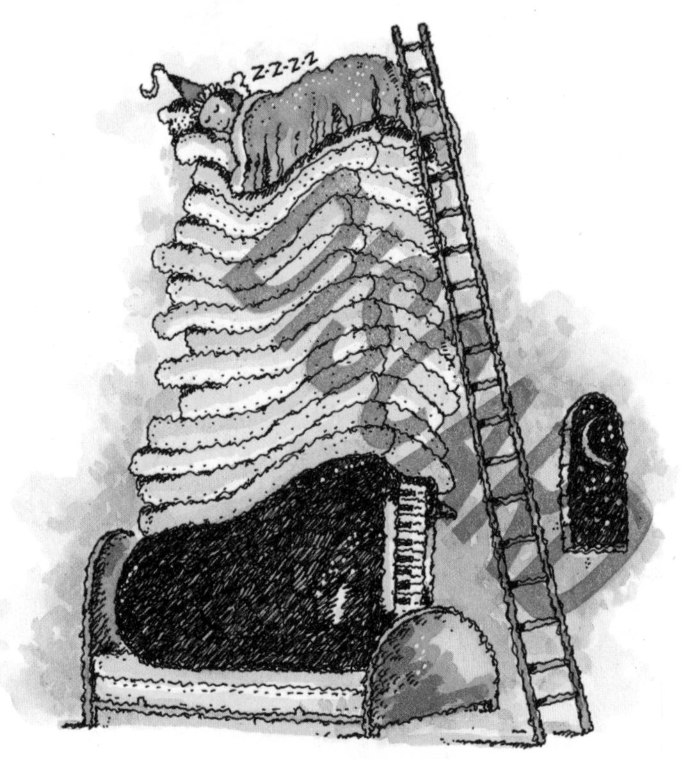

by Mike Thaler
Illustrated by Jared Lee

SCHOLASTIC INC.
New York Toronto London Auckland Sydney

For Laurel Lee Thaler,
my true princess
at last!
— M.T.

To P.J.,
Wife. Friend. Babe.
— J.L.

ISBN 0-590-89825-6

Library of Congress Catalog Card Number: 95-73254.

12 11 10 9 8 7 6 5 4 3 2 9/9 0 1 2/0

Printed in the U.S.A. 24

First Scholastic printing, March 1997

Once upon a time there was a prince
who was eager to be married.
But his parents wouldn't let him marry just anyone.
Only a *true* princess would do.

Now, true princesses are super sensitive.
They are not sound sleepers.
The slightest little lump or bump in the bed
can keep a true princess up all night.

So, every time a princess stayed at the castle,
the queen put a tiny *pea*
under 20 queen-sized mattresses.
The princess who couldn't sleep
would be the girl for her son.

Many beautiful princesses did spend the night,
for the king and queen ran a bed-and-breakfast,
just to make ends meet.

Clean towels?
How'd you like your eggs?

At breakfast the queen would casually
ask each princess how she had slept.
And they all would answer:
"Great.
Like a log.
Never better!"

"Drat!" said the prince each time.

He did everything he could to wake up a princess.
He blasted rock and roll on his stereo.
He practiced his drums.
He did roof repairs, all to no avail.

Z-Z-Z-Z

Finally, he threw out all the queen's peas
and began to place bigger items under the mattresses.
One night he slipped in a *pea-nut*.

The next morning, Princess #95
skipped down to breakfast.
"How'd you sleep, my dear?" asked the king and queen.
"Great.
Like a log.
Never better!"

"Double drat!" said the prince.
The next night he stuffed a *pea-napple* under the mattresses.

But in the morning,
Princess #96 gave the usual perky reply:
"Great.
Like a log.
Never better!"

That's when the desperate prince
crammed a *pea-ano* under the mattresses.

That night, Princess #97 climbed into bed, shut her eyes, and fell fast asleep.

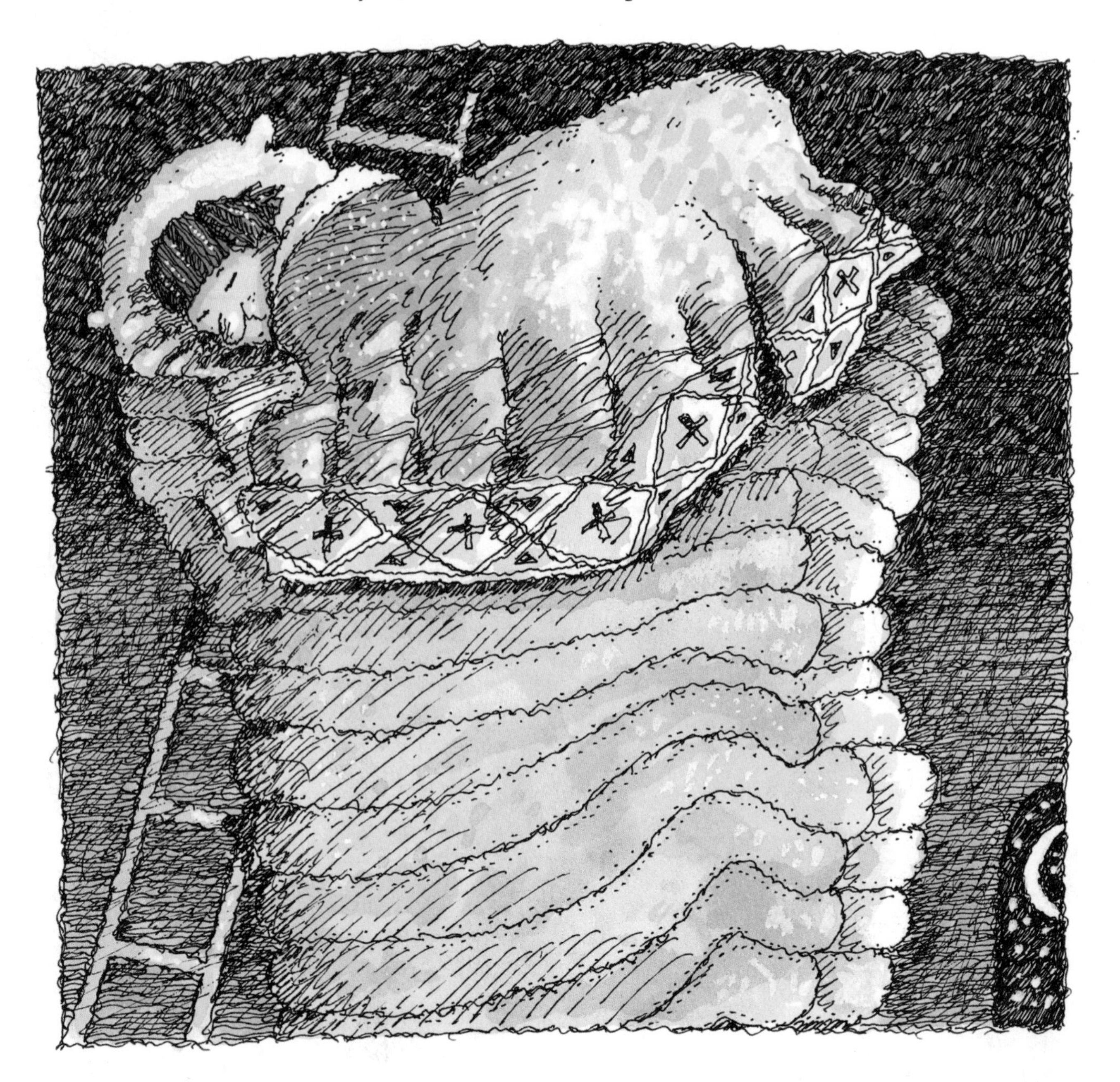

She snored all night,
and it took six servants
to wake her in the morning.

Shake her again, boys!

"How'd you sleep?" asked everybody.
"Great.
Like a log.
Never better!"
said the princess, stretching.
"Didn't you feel *anything*?" prompted the prince.
"Not a thing," piped the princess.

"What's your name?"
asked the prince, nearly in tears.
"Sleeping Beauty," she said with a nod,
dozing off again and
falling facedown into her porridge.

The prince, who knew his fairy tales,
raised her head out of the bowl
and kissed her.

Sleeping Beauty woke up.
"I can't sleep," she complained.
"This oatmeal is too lumpy."

"Sensitive!" said the king and queen.
"My true princess at last!" shouted the prince.

"Sleeping Beauty, will you marry me before lunch?"
he proposed.
"If I can wash my face first,"
she replied.

So they were married that very morning.

After the honeymoon, Sleeping Beauty became a mattress tester for *Royal Snooze* mattresses,

but was fired two days later …

for sleeping on the job.